RIDER WOOFSON

MYSTERY MOUNTAIN GETAWAY

BY WALKER STYLES **ILLUSTRATED BY BEN WHITEHOUSE**

LITTLE SIMON

New York   London   Toronto   Sydney   New Delhi

LITTLE SIMON

An imprint of Simon & Schuster Children's Publishing Division
1230 Avenue of the Americas, New York, New York 10020
First Little Simon hardcover edition October 2017
Copyright © 2017 by Simon & Schuster, Inc.
Also available in a Little Simon paperback edition. All rights reserved, including the right of reproduction in whole or in part in any form. LITTLE SIMON is a registered trademark of Simon & Schuster, Inc., and associated colophon is a trademark of Simon & Schuster, Inc.
For information about special discounts for bulk purchases, please contact Simon & Schuster Special Sales at 1-866-506-1949 or business@simonandschuster.com.
The Simon & Schuster Speakers Bureau can bring authors to your live event. For more information or to book an event contact the Simon & Schuster Speakers Bureau at 1-866-248-3049 or visit our website at www.simonspeakers.com.
Designed by Laura Roode. The text of this book was set in ITC American Typewriter.
Manufactured in the United States of America 0917 FFG
2 4 6 8 10 9 7 5 3 1
This book has been cataloged with the Library of Congress.
ISBN 978-1-4814-9895-1 (pbk)
ISBN 978-1-4814-9896-8 (hc)
ISBN 978-1-4814-9897-5 (eBook)

CONTENTS

chapter
ONE

TIME FOR A VACATION!

"P.I. Pack, we need to talk," Rider Woofson said. Rider was Pawston's best detective. His team—the Pup Investigators Pack—was made up of three other dog detectives. They gathered around their boss in the office. Rider seemed very serious.

The others were ready for bad news. Was there a jewelry heist?

Was there a bank robbery?

Instead, Rider smiled. "I have decided we need a vacation!"

"Hooray!" Ziggy Fluffenscruff yipped. He was the young detective with an amazing nose.

"Brilliant!" noted Westie Barker, the team's inventor.

"Well, it's about time," added Rora Gooddog, who was Rider's second-in-command.

"I'm glad you agree," Rider said, handing out some travel brochures for different vacation spots. "Now all we need to do is decide where we want to go."

"How about a tropical beach?" asked Rora.

"Well, we just came back from a beach where we nabbed the Sunburn Bandit," Westie said. He pointed to his red face. "I've had a little *too* much sun. Perhaps we could explore the ocean in an underwater submarine?"

"But then we also just got back from putting the Smelly Jellyfish behind bars," Rora said. She shook her head and water flew all over the office. "I am still drying off. What about an old-west ghost town?"

Ziggy was shocked. "Are you even listening to yourself? There's no way I'm going to a *ghost* town."

Rider smiled. "This is exactly why we need a vacation. We've been working hard and catching bad guys. Now we need to catch some time to relax."

"Hmm, what's the opposite of sunny, underwater, and the Wild West?" Rora asked.

"Snow, mountains, and peace and quiet," Ziggy said.

"Ziggy, you're a genius!" said
Westie. He, Rora, and Rider unfolded
one of the travel brochures.

"I am?" Ziggy asked, hopping
up and down trying to see which
vacation getaway the others were
looking at.

"How do you feel about skiing?"
Rora smiled.

"You mean log cabins and fire-
places and hot cocoa?" Ziggy said.
"I'm in! Good-bye, criminals! Hello,
vacation!"

chapter TWO

INTO THE MOUNTAINS

The detectives packed their coats and warmest socks. Then they hopped into the van and left for their vacation. On the way, they looked at a map of Mystery Mountain.

"A hundred years ago, they searched for gold here," Westie said. "There isn't any left now, so animals come here for the lodges and ski slopes."

"Who cares about old gold?" Rora said. She held up her laptop. "Check out the different diamond-level ski slopes we can ride."

"Did you say diamonds?" Ziggy asked with a sparkle in his eye. "If we find diamonds, I can trade them for food! Think of all the s'mores, and snow cones, and pies, and ice-cream cakes. Then I'd wash it all

down with hot chocolate."

"Actually, *diamonds* are used as a symbol for types of ski slopes," Rora explained.

Ziggy wasn't listening. He kept talking about food. "I'd have pasta and sandwiches and pizzas. Those would be great appetizers. Then it's on to the main course."

"Someone sure loves to think with his stomach,"

Rider said with a smile. "What are you working on back there, Westie?"

Westie was in the back of the van, tinkering with his latest invention. "Oh, just some Snow-Jets. Put them on skis and you can speed down every slope. It'll be the fastest vacation ever!"

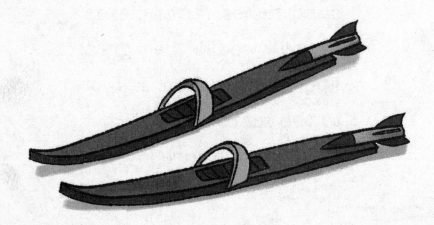

"Speaking of fast," Rider said, "we might even be able to hit the slopes today. There's no traffic."

"It looks like all the cars are driving *down* the mountain," Rora said. "That's odd. I thought everyone would be going *up* for the weekend."

"More food for us!" Ziggy said.

The P.I. Pack drove under a large wooden sign that said WELCOME TO MYSTERY MOUNTAIN.

Just as they pulled up to the lodge, other guests were hopping into their cars and leaving.

"Hmm, I wonder where everyone is going," Rider said.

Rora watched as the last car drove away. "Where did you hear about this place?"

"From Mr. Meow, believe it or not," said Rider. "It's his favorite getaway. I figured if a rich cat like him loved it, it must be nice."

"Oh no," Ziggy whined. "I smell a mystery."

chapter
THREE

THE HAUNTED SNOWBOT

The four detectives walked inside the Mystery Mountain Ski Lodge. "It's too quiet," Ziggy said. "It's kind of creepy."

"Don't worry, kid," Rora said. "We'll be out skiing all day."

DING! Rider rang the bell at the front desk.

"Hello there!" said a monkey

who popped up from behind the desk. She wore a thick sweater with a smiley face on it. She also wore diamond earrings, a diamond necklace, and a diamond name tag that said MONICA MONKIKI, OWNER. "I thought all our guests had left. You must be on your way out."

"Actually, we'd like to check in," Rider said. "We'd like four rooms for the weekend."

"You do?!" Monica seemed surprised. "I mean, we'd love for you to stay, but with everything that's going on . . . well, I figured no one would be visiting for a while!"

"What's going on?" Rora asked.

"You didn't hear?" Monica hopped up on the front desk and leaned in to whisper to the detectives. "There's a haunted Snowbot around these parts. He's half–abominable snowman and half-robot. He's been scaring away all

our skiers on the slopes. One minute he springs from the trees, and the next minute he vanishes into thin air. I have heard he can even walk through walls!"

"Okay, thanks for the warning." Ziggy turned for the exit. "We'll be heading home now."

"A Snowbot?" Westie said as he rubbed his chin. "Fascinating!"

"Usually business is booming," Monica continued. "The rooms are always booked; the mountains are crowded with skiers; and everyone is happy. But a few months ago, a movie crew came to the lodge to shoot a new film. It was about a super-skier and his best friend, a Snowbot."

Ziggy turned back around to the front desk. "Hey, I wanted to see that movie!"

Monica nodded. "Well, the movie had to close down because someone stole all of their equipment. Even the Snowbot went missing, and it was a one-of-a-kind robot made just for the movie."

"That's terrible," Westie said.

"That's not the worst part," Monica added. "Last week, the Snowbot returned. He's been chasing off everyone since, so I

understand if you'd like to leave
too."

"Great idea," Ziggy said, turn-
ing for the exit again.

Rora grabbed his suspenders.
"Hold on, kid. If there's a mystery
here, then we should solve it."

"I agree," Rider said.

"I'd like to see this Snowbot for myself, too," said Westie.

"Oh no!" Monica said. "It's far too dangerous. You should go home now. You'll stay safer that way."

"Listen to the smart monkey!" Ziggy said, but the others shook their heads.

"This is what we do, ma'am," Rider said. "We're detectives."

"Even on our days off," Rora added.

"But first, can we see our rooms and order some room service?" Ziggy begged.

"Of course, if you really want to stay." Monica scowled and hit the bell on the desk twice. *DING DING!*

A giant gorilla came out in a bellhop uniform. His name tag read GRUMPY GUS, BELLHOP.

"I'll take your luggage and show you to your rooms."

Ziggy whispered to the others, "I bet he's the bad guy. Mystery solved. Can we have fun now?"

The others shook their heads and said, "No."

chapter
FOUR

ROOM SERVICE

Rider, Rora, and Westie had been knocking on Ziggy's door for fifteen minutes.

"Hmm, perhaps he went skiing already?" suggested Westie.

"I have an idea." Rider knocked once more and said, "Room service!"

"I'm here! I'm here!"

Ziggy's pawsteps echoed as he rushed to the door. "Did you bring the chocolate jelly-bone basket—hey! You're not room service!"

"No, we're your fellow detectives, waiting on *you* to help solve a case," Rora said. She peeked into Ziggy's room. It was covered with empty food carts, trays, and plates. Ziggy was wearing a bib and holding a bowl of pasta.

"Do I have to go? I bet you could solve this on your own," Ziggy whined. "Plus, this pasta isn't going to eat itself!"

"The pasta can wait, Ziggy," Rider said. "We can't do this without you."

"Fine, give me one second." The young pup closed the door, and opened it one second later. He was not only dressed, he was overdressed. He wore two coats, three scarves, two pairs of gloves, two pairs of socks, and two pairs of pants.

"Aren't you going to be a little warm with all that on?" Westie asked.

"Better too hot than too cold," Ziggy said.

Out on the slopes, the P.I. Pack hopped onto the ski lift. As it rose into the air and up the mountain, Ziggy grabbed the rail. "This thing doesn't seem safe at all."

"Oh, it's very safe," Westie said.
"See? The control room is right
there."

"Look. Grumpy Gus is running
the ski lift," Rora noted. "He's the
bellhop *and* the ski lift controller?
I wonder what other jobs he has
around here."

"There is nothing wrong with working hard," Rider said. "Now keep your eyes and noses alert, gang. We can scan the entire mountain for clues from up here."

"I can't see a thing," Ziggy said. "This snow is too bright!"

"That's because the sun is reflecting off the snow," Westie

explained. "See? The Triple Black Diamond course is shining the brightest. But we'll never ride that slope. It's the hardest one on the mountain. I'll stick to the bunny slope."

"Wow! There's a special slope for bunnies?" Ziggy asked.

Westie chuckled. "No, the bunny slope is what we call an easy slope for beginners."

"Have you two spotted any clues yet?" Rider asked.

"Yeah, I see something really

important!" Ziggy cheered and practically leaped out of his seat. "It's the snack bar!"

"You're right, kid," Rora said. "Next to the snack bar— it's the Snowbot, and he's skiing away!"

Rider and Rora strapped their snowboards to their feet and leaped off as the ski lift arrived at the top of the mountain. Westie

had his skis while Ziggy slid on
his sled. The chase was on!

"The Snowbot is going into that
half-pipe," Rider said.

Rora zipped ahead first. She hit the half-pipe and did a triple flip. Rider followed with a double somersault. Westie went slowly around the half-pipe, and Ziggy spun around and around in circles.

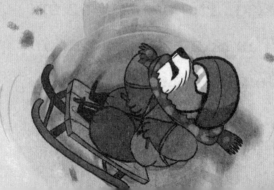

As he finally escaped the spiral, he yelped, "Someone should have warned me about that before I ate so much food!"

"The Snowbot is almost at the bottom of the slope!" Rora shouted. "He can't escape us now!"

The large, white Snowbot rode straight toward the lodge. He looked like he was going to crash

right into it. Instead, he passed
through the wall and vanished.

"Where'd he go?!" Rora asked.

Ziggy was still dizzy from the half-pipe and bumped into Westie. The pair rolled into a snowball that picked up speed as it went down the mountain. Then the snowball rolled to a stop beside the lodge.

Ziggy moaned, "Worst. Vacation. Ever."

A PRICKLY MEETING

The P.I. Pack sat inside by the fire, drinking hot chocolate to warm up.

Rider set down his mug. "Okay, it's time to find more clues."

"Maybe we should skip the half-pipes this time," Ziggy suggested.

"Actually, I was thinking we could take in some nature," Rider said. "Who wants to go on a hike?"

The hiking trail was long, cold, and beautiful. It weaved through a thick forest. As they walked, Rora spotted a log cabin hidden in the distance. They decided to check it out.

The four detectives quietly walked up to the wooden house and peeked in through the window.

"May I help you?" said a gruff voice from behind them.

Ziggy was so surprised that he jumped right into Westie's arms.

An old porcupine stood in the snow. He was wearing a flannel jacket with a pair of thick glasses

and had a long beard. He pointed
a cane at the detectives and said,
"Who are you? What do you want?"

"Don't you know sneaking up
on animals is rude!" Ziggy yipped.

"Spying on my house is rude
too," the porcupine snapped.

"We're detectives, sir," Rora
explained. "May I ask what you're
doing up here, mister?"

"I'm Piney Prince. You can call
me Old Piney. Everyone does." The
old porcupine moved to his porch,
and he took a seat in a rocking

chair. "I spend my days panning for gold in the river. What else would I be doing?"

"Gold?" Westie asked. "I thought all the gold was gone."

The porcupine nodded. "There are still tiny pieces in the river,

but Mystery Mountain used to have tons. Then, when the gold rush was over, the ski resort moved in."

Old Piney reached into his jacket and pulled out some shiny ice pellets. They sparkled in his paw. "Most days, I just find these strange icicles. They are everywhere." He tossed the ice back into the snow.

"Have you heard of the Snowbot?" Rider asked. "He's run off all the visitors."

"Snowbot?" Old Piney laughed. "What's a Snowbot?"

"It was from a movie," said Ziggy.

The porcupine stopped rocking. "Oh, I remember the movie crew. If you're working for them, then you can get their stuff off my land."

"What stuff?" Rora asked.

Old Piney shrugged. "Cameras, equipment, and machines . . . you know, stuff. It's blocking one of my favorite views. I can take you there, if you'd like."

"Yes, sir," said Rider. "We'd like that very much."

chapter
SIX

THE REAL SNOWBOT

Old Piney led the detectives up the mountain. The pack struggled with the long walk, but the old porcupine was fine.

"Do you hike a lot?" Rider asked, trying to catch his breath.

"Every day," Old Piney said. "It's so quiet and peaceful—especially when those skiers aren't here."

"Sounds like he wants the lodge closed down," Ziggy whispered to Westie. "I bet he's the bad guy."

Finally, Old Piney stopped and pointed to a collection of fancy equipment. "Here you go. I would have thrown all this stuff in the

trash, but my old back can't carry it down the mountain."

Westie inspected the gear. "Speakers, lights, microphones, cameras, tripods . . . It's everything you need to make a million-dollar movie. I bet whoever stole this is working with the Snowbot."

"Maybe the Snowbot stole it," Ziggy said. He played with a control panel and flipped a switch. Suddenly, all of the machines came to life. Lights and sounds exploded in the clearing. A real, live Snowbot walked out of the forest and roared.

"Yikes!" Ziggy cried, leaping behind Westie.

"Double-yikes!" Westie cried, leaping behind Old Piney, who poked him with his needles.

"Ouchie ouchie ouchie!" Westie cried, running in circles.

The Snowbot roared again. Rider and Rora went to grab the beast, but they went right through him!

"GHOST-BOT SNOWBOT!" Westie and Ziggy cried.

"It's no ghost!" Old Piney said as he switched off the control panel. The Snowbot vanished.

"What is going on?" Rora asked.

Westie examined the machine. "This isn't a camera at all. It's a projector! The Snowbot we just saw wasn't real."

Ziggy tried to act tough. "I knew it was fake. So fake. Just like that Snowbot mask over there." He walked over to a mask that peaked out of the forest. "This doesn't even look real."

"Uh, Ziggy . . . ," Rora said as everyone else backed away. "I wouldn't touch that if I were you."

Ziggy reached up and grabbed the mask. "This old thing is just a rubber mask that won't fool anyw*uhhhhhhagghhhh*!"

Suddenly the *very real* Snowbot lifted Ziggy into the air. Then they both roared.

Ziggy squirmed out of the Snowbot's grip and slammed into the others. They all crashed off the hill, rolling down the mountain in another giant snowball. Once again, they landed right beside the lodge.

Rider popped out and moaned, "Worst. Case. Ever."

THE WRITING'S ON THE WALL

"W-w-w-we n-n-n-need to get b-b-b-back up the m-m-m-mountain." Rider shivered in the icy weather.

"B-b-b-before the S-S-S-Snowbot gets away," Rora agreed. Her teeth chattered.

"Shouldn't you warm up first?" Grumpy Gus asked. He offered them a tray of hot chocolate.

Old Piney refused. "I don't need anything from this ski lodge." Then he walked into the forest by himself.

Grumpy Gus turned back to the others and offered them a hot drink. "Please? If you are not careful, you will catch a cold."

"No way," Rider said. "I will c-c-c-catch a c-c-c-cold if it means I'll c-c-c-catch the Snowbot, t-t-t-too."

"Well, you're n-n-n-not going b-b-b-by yourself," said Rora. "The P.I. Pack stays together."

Ziggy and Westie shivered and nodded in agreement.

The detectives hiked back up the mountain. When they arrived

at the site, all of the movie equipment was gone.

"Impossible!" said Rora. "We
weren't gone that long."

"I think Mystery Mountain just
got a little more mysterious," said
Rider.

Westie waved his phone in the air. "I'll say! Check this out. There were a lot of monsters on this mountain. And one was a porcupine!"

"Porcupine?!" Ziggy pointed out. "I told you Old Piney was the bad guy!"

"Maybe," Rora said with a sniffle. "He did say he hated the resort. Maybe he's trying to run it out of business."

"Looks like we need to pay Old Piney a visit—*ACHOO!*" Rider sneezed.

Old Piney watched the P.I. Pack through his window. "Are you sneaking around again?" he called out. "Listen, it's too cold for all this sneaking. Come inside, and let me make you some tomato soup and grilled cheese."

"You don't
have to ask me
twice!" Ziggy said.
He ran through the
front door and sat at the table.

Inside, the house was small and
cozy. There was a fire in the fire-
place, and all the furniture had
tiny holes from Old Piney's quills.

As Rora sat down, she blurted
out the question that everyone
was thinking. "Old Piney, are you
the bad guy behind the Snowbot?"

"Me? Use all that equip-
ment?" The old porcupine started

laughing. "I don't even know how to use a phone!"

"But you have been scaring all the visitors," Westie said. "We read it in the news."

"If by scaring, you mean telling those skiers to stay off my land, then sure," Old Piney said. He served the detectives their food, then sat down to eat.

"*Your* land?" Rora asked. "I thought the mountain belonged to Monica Monkiki."

"Nope," Old Piney said, dipping

the warm grilled cheese sandwich into the hot tomato soup. He pointed to the wall with his free hand.

The wall was covered in framed newspaper clippings. The articles had interesting headlines:

FOREST PRESERVE SOLD
to Build Ski Lodge

OLD PINEY STRIKES GOLD
Gets Rich and Buys Mystery Mountain

OLD PINEY DONATES SOME LAND
for Forest Preserve

SKI LODGE CUTS DOWN TREES
to Make Room for Ski Slopes

"I own all of Mystery Mountain except for the ski resort. And that's only because they tricked the Forest Preserve folks into selling," Old Piney explained. "They've been trying to get me to sell the whole mountain to them for years. I always say no."

"Why?" Rora asked.

Old Piney set down his spoon. "I love this mountain and all of its beautiful nature. I would never harm it or anyone on it. Not even those pesky skiers."

"So who is behind the Snowbot?" Ziggy asked.

"I have a hunch," Rider said. "But I just don't know what their motive is. Not yet . . ."

"What you need is some more hot soup in your tum—" Old Piney said just as a giant robot arm burst through the window and grabbed him.

chapter
EIGHT

SNOWBALL FIGHT

"After that Snowbot, P.I. Pack!" Rider shouted. "We have to save Old Piney!"

The four detectives found the porcupine's ski and sled collection and raced after the Snowbot. As they moved closer, the mechanical monster tossed Old Piney down one ski slope as it went down another.

"Time to split up!" Rider called out. "Ziggy and Rora, save Old Piney! Westie, let's grab the Snowbot."

Ziggy leaned a sled down the left slope while Rora skied right beside him. They weaved through the trees as Old Piney tumbled in the soft snow. Finally, they caught Old Piney and tossed him on the back of the sled.

"I've got you!" Ziggy cheered.

"But who's got you?" Old Piney asked as the sled hit a ski jump. The three of them flew through the air and landed in a giant, rolling snowball.

"Not again!" Ziggy and Rora cried.

Meanwhile, on the other ski slope, Rider rode a snowboard and zipped after the Snowbot. Westie had put his Snow-Jets onto a pair of skis.

"I'll get him, Boss!" Westie said as he flipped on the switch. *ZOOM!* The tiny jets blasted to life, but they sent Westie rocketing *up* the mountain instead of *down!* "Yikes! I have them in reverse!"

Westie flipped another switch and the skis blasted forward. Now he was zooming in the right direction, but he was going way too fast. First he passed Rider. Then he passed the Snowbot, who looked very surprised. Westie was heading for a massive ski jump, but the Snow-Jets ran out of energy. He slid to a stop, but the Snowbot didn't. It hit the jump and landed in a tree.

Springs and wires flew everywhere. Rider pulled alongside
Westie. "It really was a robot."

"Of course it was," Westie said.
"But who was controlling it?"

"We need to get back to the lodge to find out," said Rider.

As Rider and Westie reached the bottom of the mountain, the Ziggy-Rora-Piney snowball rolled right into the side of the lodge. Monica and Grumpy Gus rushed outside.

Monica pointed to Old Piney. "You are scaring my guests." Then she found a device in the snow next to him. "What's this?"

"That's the remote control for the Snowbot!" Westie exclaimed.

"Looks like we have our bad guy," Monica said. "Case closed."

chapter
NINE

BACKWARD SKI

After the police took Old Piney away, the detectives met in Rider's room. "This doesn't feel right," Rider said.

"They got the wrong guy," Rora said.

"Seriously," Ziggy agreed. "Bad guys can't make grilled cheese *that* delicious. It's impossible!"

"We did catch Old Piney with the remote control for the Snowbot," said Westie.

Rider paced back and forth. "I need some time to think."

The others watched as he went outside to skate on the frozen pond.

"Um, what's he doing?" Ziggy asked.

"He's ice-rink-thinking," Rora said. "If anyone can figure this out, it's Rider. I hope."

As he twirled gracefully over the ice, Rider was also spinning a plan to catch the true criminal.

The next morning, the P.I. Pack met for breakfast. Monica served them and asked how they had slept.

"Terribly," Rider complained. "I could hear the Snowbot all night!"

"That is . . . impossible," Monica said. "The Snowbot mystery was solved!"

Ziggy shook his head. "I heard him too."

Then Rora pointed out of the

window. "Well I see the Snowbot skiing on the hill right now!"

"Impossible!" Monica cried again. "I . . . I . . ."

"You what?" Rora asked.

"I . . . I'll catch him myself!" Monica shouted.

"Here, use my skis," Rider said with a smile.

Monica raced outside, put on the

skis, and chased after the Snowbot. They slid through slaloms and flew through the air. She was hot on the tail of the Snowbot, but when she reached it, the Snowbot vanished.

"Where'd that machine go?" Monica yelled from the slopes. She looked back at the lodge and saw

Westie on the top floor holding the movie crew's projector. He had been projecting the Snowbot.

Rider stepped out of the woods next to Monica. "There's s*now* need to make up a story anymore. We know that *you* controlled the Snowbot!"

"You'll never catch me!" Monica darted toward the black diamond course and zoomed down the slope. She had an escape snowmobile hidden at bottom. But Rider didn't chase her. Instead, he flipped a switch on the remote control for Westie's Snow-Jets that were attached to the skis that he had given to Monica.

Suddenly, the monkey stopped

going *down* the black diamond
slope, and started going back *up*—
in reverse.

"Argghhhhhh!" she screamed. The skis blasted her right into the same tree where the Snowbot had been stuck. A sprinkling of strange, bright icicles tumbled down from her snow-covered outfit. Rider held out his paw to catch them.

"It seems like we've gotten to the root of this problem," he said with a smile. "Monica Monkiki, you are under arrest."

A GOOD ~~GOLD~~ OLD ENDING

The police returned to arrest the real criminal, Monica Monkiki, and to release Old Piney.

"Hmm, I don't understand any of this," Old Piney said.

"I'm happy to explain," Rider said. He was about to pat the porcupine on the back but then thought better of it.

"Mystery Mountain is actually a mixture of snow and *diamonds*. When Monica discovered this, she tried to buy the whole mountain from you. But, of course, you wouldn't sell. So she tried to scare everyone away, but she made it look like you were the one doing it. She made up lots of monsters, like the

Evil Elf, the Risky Reindeer, and, of course, the Haunted Snowbot. If she could frame you for creating the monsters, then you would go to jail while she collected all the diamonds."

"But how'd you figure it out?" Old Piney asked.

"When we first checked in, I found it odd that the owner wore so many diamonds," Rider explained. "Then you showed us the weird icicles you kept finding. I realize now that those were also diamonds. But the final clue came when Monica tried to frame you with the remote. You shared your cabin, your food, and your kindness with us. We knew you weren't the bad guy!"

"What about the gorilla, Grumpy Gus? Was he part of it too?" Ziggy asked.

"No," Rider said. "He's just grumpy."

"That's true," Grumpy Gus said gruffly as he brought the guests more hot chocolate.

"But why scare off the skiers from her lodge?" Old Piney asked.

"Because they wanted my diamonds!" Monica screamed from the back of the police car. "It was only a matter of time before the skiers discovered the diamonds on this mountain. I wanted them all

for myself! Then that pesky movie crew came, and they were going to find the diamonds. So I had to get rid of them, too!"

Rora smiled. "She used the Snowbot to scare them. We found the missing equipment in her lodge."

"Wait a minute. Those icicles I've been tossing out are honest-to-goodness diamonds, and I've been looking for *gold* all this time?!" Old Piney laughed. "Well, I'll be a Snowbot's uncle."

The dog detectives laughed.

"Thank you for your help, P.I. Pack," said Old Piney. "You're welcome back here any time."

"Thank you," said Rider. "This has sure been an action-packed vacation."

"What vacation?" Rora asked. "We worked the whole time!"

"Hmm," Westie said. "Maybe

we could take one more run down the ski slope?"

"And maybe I could order one or two or fifty more things from room service!" Ziggy said.

"Sorry, P.I. Pack," Rider said. "It's time to head back to Pawston. Crime never takes a vacation."

CHECK OUT RIDER WOOFSON'S NEXT CASE!

Flash! A large camera took a picture of the P.I. Pack office as if it were a crime scene. The photographer was a kangaroo. He hopped around the office, taking more pictures. *Flash! Flash!*

"Hey! What's *hopping*—I mean, happening around here?" Westie Barker asked. The furry inventor

Excerpt from *The Very First Case*

pointed to a sign. "This area is top secret! Who are you?"

"Relax, Westie," said lead detective Rider Woofson. "This is Scoops Hopper. He's a reporter from the *Pawston Paw Print* newspaper. He's writing a story on the P.I. Pack."

"Nice to meet you," Scoops said. He held up his camera and snapped another picture. *Flash!*

Westie rubbed his eyes. "I wish I could say the same."

"Don't mind Mr. Science. He's camera-shy." It was Ziggy, the team's youngest detective. "Not me though! Go ahead. Snap away. What kind of story are you doing about Pawston's greatest detectives? Let me guess. Is it one about the time we battled Icy Ivan, the evil Penguin Prowler? Good thing I brought my appetite. I saved the day by eating my way out of an Ice Cream, You Scream trap!"